Russell Hoban

How Tom Beat Captain Najork and his Hired Sportsmen

Illustrated by Quentin Blake

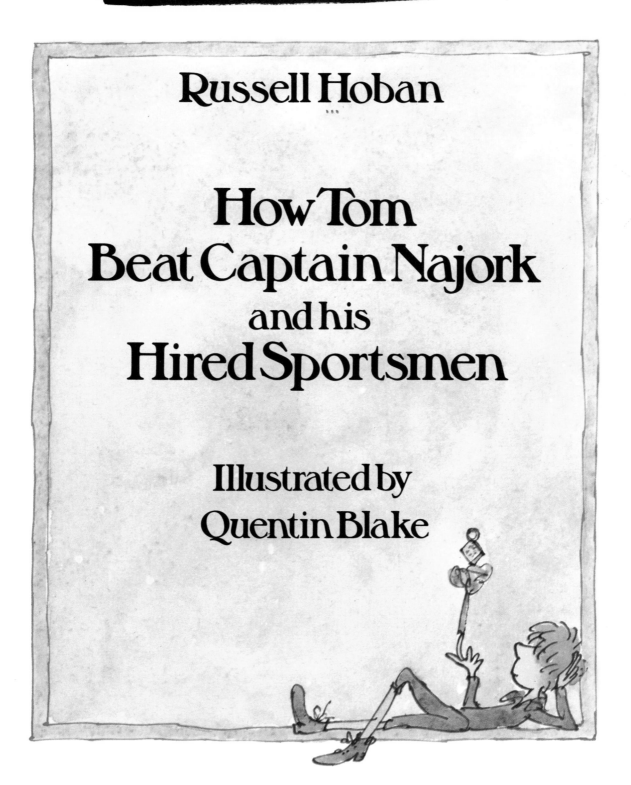

Atheneum 1974 New York

Library of Congress Cataloging in Publication Data

Hoban, Russell.
   How Tom beat Captain Najork and his hired sportsmen.

   SUMMARY: Because Tom's aunt disapproves of his
constant fooling around she calls in Captain Najork to
teach him a lesson. Tom, however, has a splendid idea.
   I. Blake, Quentin, illus. II. Title.
PZ7.H637Ho   [Fic]   74-75573
ISBN 0-689-30441-2

Tom lived with his maiden aunt, Miss Fidget Wonkham-Strong.
She wore an iron hat, and took no nonsense from anyone.
Where she walked the flowers drooped, and when she sang the
trees all shivered.

Tom liked to fool around. He fooled around with sticks and stones and crumpled paper, with mewses and passages and dustbins, with bent nails and broken glass and holes in fences.

He fooled around with mud, and stomped and squelched and slithered through it.

He fooled around on high-up things that shook and wobbled and teetered.

He fooled around with dropping things from bridges into rivers and fishing them out.

He fooled around with barrels in alleys.

When Aunt Fidget Wonkham-Strong asked him what
he was doing, Tom said that he was fooling around.

"It looks very like playing to me," said Aunt Fidget
Wonkham-Strong. "Too much playing is not good, and you play
too much. You had better stop it and do something useful."

"All right," said Tom.

But he did not stop. He did a little fooling around with two or three cigar bands and a paper-clip.

At dinner Aunt Fidget Wonkham-Strong, wearing her iron hat, said, "Eat your mutton and your cabbage-and-potato sog." "All right," said Tom. He ate it.

After dinner Aunt Fidget Wonkham-Strong said, "Now learn off pages 65 to 75 of the Nautical Almanac, and that will teach you not to fool around so much." "All right," said Tom. He learned them off.

"From now on I shall keep an eye on you," Aunt Fidget Wonkham-Strong said, "and if you do not stop fooling around I shall send for Captain Najork and his hired sportsmen."

"Who is Captain Najork?" said Tom.

"Captain Najork," said Aunt Fidget Wonkham-Strong, "is seven feet tall, with eyes like fire, a voice like thunder, and a handlebar moustache. His trousers are always freshly pressed, his blazer is immaculate, his shoes are polished mirror-bright, and he is every inch a terror. When Captain Najork is sent for he comes up the river in his pedal boat, with his hired sportsmen all pedalling hard. He teaches fooling-around boys the lesson they so badly need, and it is not one that they soon forget."

Aunt Fidget Wonkham-Strong kept an eye on Tom. He did not stop fooling around. He did low and muddy fooling around and he did high and wobbly fooling around. He fooled around with dropping things off bridges and he fooled around with barrels in alleys.

"Very well," said Aunt Fidget Wonkham-Strong at table in her iron hat. "Eat your greasy bloaters."

Tom ate them.

"I have warned you," said Aunt Fidget Wonkham-Strong, "that I should send for Captain Najork if you did not stop fooling around. I have done that. As you like to play so much, you shall play against Captain Najork and his hired sportsmen. They play hard games and they play them jolly hard. Prepare yourself."

"All right," said Tom. He fooled around with a bottle-top
and a burnt match.

The next day Captain Najork came up the river with his hired sportsmen pedalling his pedal boat.

They came ashore smartly, carrying an immense brown-paper parcel. They marched into the garden, one, two, three, four. Captain Najork was only six feet tall. His eyes were not like fire, his voice was not like thunder.

"Right," said Captain Najork. "Where is the sportive infant?"

"There," said Aunt Fidget Wonkham-Strong.

"Here," said Tom.

"Right," said the Captain. "We shall play womble, muck, and sneedball, in that order." The hired sportsmen sniggered as they undid the immense brown-paper parcel, set up the womble run, the ladders and the net, and distributed the rakes and stakes.

"How do you play womble?" said Tom.

"You'll find out," said Captain Najork.

"Who's on my side?" said Tom.

"Nobody," said Captain Najork. "Let's get started."

Womble turned out to be a shaky, high-up, wobbling and teetering sort of a game, and Tom was used to that kind of fooling around. The Captain's side raked first. Tom staked. The hired sportsmen played so hard that they wombled too fast, and were shaky with the rakes. Tom fooled around the way he always did, and all his stakes dropped true. When it was his turn to rake he did not let Captain Najork and the hired sportsmen score a single rung, and at the end of the snetch he won by six ladders.

"Right," said Captain Najork, clenching his teeth. "Muck next. Same sides."

The court was laid out at low tide in the river mud. Tom mucked first, and slithered through the marks while the hired sportsmen poled and shovelled. Tom had fooled around with mud so much that he scored time after time.

Captain Najork's men poled too hard and shovelled too fast and
tired themselves out. Tom just mucked about and fooled around,
and when the tide came in he led the opposition 673 to 49.

"Really," said Aunt Fidget Wonkham-Strong to Captain
Najork, "you must make an effort to teach this boy a lesson."

"Some boys learn hard," said the Captain, chewing his
moustache. "Now for sneedball."

The hired sportsmen brought out the ramp, the slide, the
barrel, the bobble, the sneeding tongs, the bar, and the grapples.
Tom saw at once that sneedball was like several kinds of fooling
around that he was particularly good at. Partly it was like
dropping things off bridges into rivers and fishing them out and
partly it was like fooling around with barrels in alleys.

"I had better tell you," said the Captain to Tom, "that I
played in the Sneedball Finals five years running."

"They couldn't have been very final if you had to keep doing
it for five years," said Tom. He motioned the Captain aside,
away from Aunt Fidget Wonkham-Strong. "Let's make this
interesting," he said.

"What do you mean?" said the Captain.

"Let's play *for* something," said Tom. "Let's say if I win I get your pedal boat."

"What do I get if *I* win?" said the Captain. "Because I am certainly going to win *this* one."

"You can have Aunt Fidget Wonkham-Strong," said Tom.

"She's impressive," said the Captain. "I admit that freely. A very impressive lady."

"She fancies you," said Tom. "I can tell by the way she looks sideways at you from underneath her iron hat."

"No!" said the Captain.

"Yes," said Tom.

"And you'll part with her if she'll have me?" said the Captain.

"It's the only sporting thing to do," said Tom.

"Agreed then!" said the Captain. "By George! I'm almost sorry that I'm going to have to teach you a lesson by beating you at sneedball."

"Let's get started," said Tom.

The hired sportsmen had first slide. Captain Najork himself barrelled, and he and his men played like demons. But Tom tonged the bobble in the same fooling-around way that he fished things out of rivers, and he quickly moved into the lead. Captain Najork sweated big drops, and he slid his barrel too hard so it hit the stop and slopped over. But Tom just fooled around, and when it was his slide he never spilled a drop.

Darkness fell, but they shot up flares and went on playing. By three o'clock in the morning Tom had won by 85 to 10. As the last flare went up above the garden he looked down from the ramp at the defeated Captain and his hired sportsmen and he said, "Maybe that will teach you not to fool around with a boy who knows how to fool around."

Captain Najork broke down and wept, but Aunt Fidget Wonkham-Strong had him put to bed and brought him peppermint tea, and then he felt better.

Tom took his boat and pedalled
to the next town down the
river. There he advertised
in the newspaper for a new aunt.
When he found one that he liked,
he told her, "No greasy
bloaters, no mutton and no
cabbage-and-potato sog. No
Nautical Almanac. And I do lots
of fooling around. Those are
my conditions."

The new aunt's name was Bundlejoy Cosysweet. She had a
floppy hat with flowers on it. She had long, long hair.
 "That sounds fine to me," she said. "We'll have a go."

Aunt Fidget Wonkham-Strong married Captain Najork even though he had lost the sneedball game, and they were very happy together. She made the hired sportsmen learn off pages of the Nautical Almanac every night after dinner.

E   Hoban
COP.2   How Tom beat Captain
           Najork and his hired
           sportsmen

DATE DUE			
JAN 19 1995			
FEB 06 1995			

G.I. JOE

A REAL AMERICAN HERO

VOLUME 2

G.I. JOE: A REAL AMERICAN HERO, VOLUME 2

Writer: **Larry Hama**

Artist: **S L Gallant**

Inker: **Gary Erskine**

Colorist: **J. Brown**

Letters: **Shawn Lee**

Series Editor: **Carlos Guzman**

Collection Editor: **Justin Eisinger**

Collection Designer: **Chris Mowry**

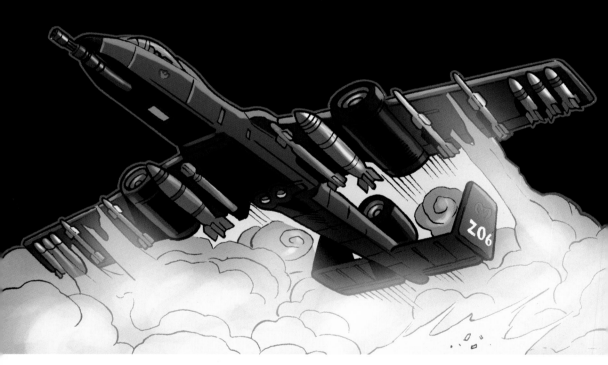

Special thanks to Hasbro's Aaron Archer, Michael Kelly, Amie Lozanski, Ed Lane, Joe Furfaro, Jos Huxley, Samantha Lomow, and Michael Verrecchia for their invaluable assistance.

ISBN: 978-1-60010-941-6

20 19 18 17   2 3 4 5

Licensed By: Hasbro

Ted Adams, CEO & Publisher
Greg Goldstein, Chief Operating Officer
Robbie Robbins, EVP/Sr. Graphic Artist
Chris Ryall, Chief Creative Officer/Editor-in-Chief
Matthew Ruzicka, CPA, Chief Financial Officer
Alan Payne, VP of Sales

Become our fan on Facebook **facebook.com/idwpublishing**
Follow us on Twitter **@idwpublishing**
Check us out on YouTube **youtube.com/idwpublishing**
www.IDWPUBLISHING.com

THE INTEL ON THIS PLACE HAD BETTER BE RIGHT. HOW DO WE KNOW THAT STORM SHADOW IS *REALLY* BACK ON OUR SIDE AGAIN?

WE DON'T HAVE ANY CHOICE, CLUTCH...

THAT'S RIGHT, LADY JAYE...

...IF THERE'S EVEN AN OUTSIDE CHANCE OF COBRA HOLDING CHUCKLES HOSTAGE HERE IN SPRINGFIELD, WE HAVE TO TRY TO GET HIM OUT.

GOOD POINT, GUNG-HO.

MAN, WHEN COBRA ABANDONED THIS BURG, THEY MOVED OUT LOCK, STOCK, AND BARREL!

SLOW DOWN, CLUTCH...

...WE HAVE TO HOOK A LEFT AT THE NEXT CORNER.

—ALL I'M REQUIRED TO TELL YOU IS MY NAME, RANK, AND SERIAL NUMBER...

...BUT I'M NOT EVEN GIVING YOU LOSERS THE SATISFACTION OF TELLING YOU *ANYTHING.*

YOU'LL TELL US PLENTY AS SOON AS I FINISH SOAKING THIS TELEPHONE BOOK.

WE ALREADY KNOW YOUR NAME, *CHUCKLES*—AND WHO CARES ABOUT YOUR RANK AND SERIAL NUMBER?

WHAPP

THIS IS GOING NOWHERE. THIS OPERATION IS BLOWN ANYWAY. WE SHOULD JUST POP THIS MOOK AND GET IN THE WIND. OUR RIDE SHOULD BE HERE ANY MINUTE...

4

WHAT'S TAKING THEM SO LONG? THEY ONLY HAVE ONE PRISONER TO SHOOT!

I SAY WE GIVE 'EM FIVE MINUTES AND LEAVE WITHOUT THEM!

MAN, IS THAT THE BEST YOU CAN DO? YOU MUST BE FROM THAT NEW ELITE COBRA UNIT—THE WUSS-VIPERS.

HA HA, VERY FUNNY...

SPRINGFIELD AREA LET YOUR FINGERS

...NOT!

ARE WE FINALLY GETTING TO THE GOOD PART? LET'S DO IT, RAG-FACE! LET'S BOOGIE!

TWO COBRA FIGHTING VEHICLES! WE'RE SUNK IF THEY MANEUVER TO FLANK US!

YOU TAKE OUT THE NEW MODEL HISS, CLUTCH...

VIDEO WORLD

COBRA

...ME AND LADY JAYE WILL TAKE CARE OF THE *STINGER!*

IT'S THE *JOES!*

I'LL CONCENTRATE FIRE ON THEIR VEHICLE...

BRRRAPPP

...YOU GUYS IN THE *STINGER* DEAL WITH THE TWO THAT ARE HEADING FOR THE ARCADE!

C'MON, COBRAS—TAKE THE *BAIT!*

THIS SHOULD BE EASY—

WHUMP

WHUMP

THAT *VAMP* IS AT A DISADVANTAGE! WITHOUT A GUNNER, THE DRIVER HAS TO *STOP* TO ENGAGE US!

SMART MOVE, FORGETTING TO TIE UP MY *FEET*, TWINKLETOES!

OOF!

THAT'S THE WAY TO THE BASEMENT, BUT I DON'T THINK EVEN *YOU* CAN KICK DOWN A STEEL DOOR LIKE THAT!

MAYBE NOT...

—AND THIS IS FOR THE WET PHONEBOOK!

BONK

...BUT A 40 MIKE-MIKE GRENADE CAN!

LAISSEZ LE BON TEMPS ROULER!

THUMP

WHAMM

UNG!

IT'S ABOUT TIME!

WHOOOM

HE'S GETTING IN RANGE! IF HE CORRECTS AND BRACKETS THE NEXT SHOTS, I AM *MEAT!*

TIME TO FLIP DOWN THE HANDS-FREE LASER SIGHT...

SYSTEM ARMED

INCOMING FIRE

...ACQUIRE TARGET AND LOCK-ON—

—AND SWITCH TO VOICE-ACTIVATION TRIGGER.

"BANG!"

THOOM

SCRATCH ONE *HISS* TANK.

KA-WHAMM

MA'S—THIS ONE STOPPED A STEEL DOOR WITH HIS BODY... I THINK HE'S OUT FOR THE COUNT.

I'LL CUT CHUCKLES LOOSE!

FORGET ABOUT ME, *SHOOT* THIS GUY! DOUBLE TAP HIM!

LOOK, I KNOW YOU'RE ANGRY, BUT—

GIMME—

—THAT!

KA-POW

I'M GOING TO HAVE TO TAKE YOU INTO CUSTODY, CHUCKLES. THAT WAS BEYOND THE PALE...

KACHUK

ANGER HAD NOTHING TO DO WITH IT.

YOU'RE WELCOME.

SIX HOURS LATER, IN UTAH.

FLIGHT CREW, PREPARE TO LOWER RAMP...

...WE ARE HOME.

SO, YOU GUYS HAVE BEEN GETTING THE *PIT* OUT OF MOTHBALLS?

THAT'S RIGHT. UPGRADED THE PERIMETER SECURITY WHILE WE WERE AT IT.

JABBERWOCK!

BANDERSNATCH.

OKAY, YOU'RE CLEAR, CLUTCH.

THANKS, OUTBACK.

12

YO, DUSTY.

HEY, GUNG-HO.

YOU REMEMBER THE DRILL, CHUCKLES?

I CAN HARDLY FORGET.

I GUESS IT'S BETTER THAN GETTING BEAMED DOWN, HUH?

SGT. IRON KNIFE, THE PASSWORD IS *FRABJOUS.*

THE COUNTER-SIGN IS *FRUMIOUS...*

...YOU ARE CLEARED TO ENTER.

14

"...MAINFRAME IS IN CHARGE OF THAT. HE'LL MAKE IT HAPPEN."

OKAY, WILD BILL—I'M GOING TO WALK YOU TO THE MAIN ELEVATOR.

ROGER THAT, MAINFRAME.

BEEP BIP
BEEP
BEEP
BIP

JUST A SMIDGE MORE—THE WEIGHT SENSOR WILL SOUND WHEN YOU'RE CENTERED AND THE WEIGHT DISTRIBUTION IS RIGHT.

IS THIS OKAY? I DON'T HAVE A SMIDGE-O-METER IN MY NAVIGATION CLUSTER.

THAT'S GOOD...

...YOU'RE DEAD ON! PERFECT!

BEEEEP

WIND DOWN, SET BRAKES...

...AND KEEP SEATBELTS FASTENED UNTIL THE ELEVATOR STOPS MOVING.

MESS HALL 01
CHAPEL 417
RANGE 408

OVER HERE, CHUCKLES! IN THE ELEVATOR WITH DUKE.

STALKER...

...HAS ANYBODY ELSE INTERROGATED THE SUBJECT?

STORM SHADOW HAS BEEN IN LOCK-DOWN SINCE HIS ORIGINAL DEBRIEF.

WE NEED TO FIND OUT IF STORM SHADOW IS ON THE LEVEL, OR IF HE IS AN UNWILLING DOUBLE AGENT, OR SOME SORT OF SLEEPER. AND WE HAVE TO DO IT BY THE *BOOK*.

ARE YOU OKAY WITH THAT?

I DON'T DO RENDITIONS, DUKE. THERE'S NO SENATE COMMITTEE LOOKING OVER OUR SHOULDERS ON THIS ONE, IS THERE?

I DIDN'T FIGURE YOU WERE FLYING HIM TO TRUCIAL ABYSMIA, CHUCKLES. AND THE REASON WE DO THINGS THE RIGHT WAY ISN'T BECAUSE SOMEBODY IS LOOKING.

SECURITY AREA'S STILL THE SAME, RIGHT?

YES, BUT I'D BE CAREFUL GOING THROUGH THAT DOOR—

ATTENTION HIGH SECURITY HOLDING CELL

HOLD IT RIGHT THERE, BUB!

SCARLETT! HEY, I'M CLEARED FOR THIS SECTION—

YOU JUST FIND OUT EVERYTHING WE NEED TO KNOW TO GET SNAKE EYES BACK!

AND YOU HAD BETTER NOT MESS UP!

OKAY, LET'S LET THE MAN GO AHEAD AND DO HIS JOB, SHALL WE?

NOT TOO MUCH PRESSURE FOR YOU, CHUCKLES?

I CAN HANDLE IT.

ROADBLOCK IS RUNNING SECURITY HERE, BUT PSYCHE-OUT IS HONCHO OF THIS LOCK-DOWN SECTION.

AND AS SUCH, I AM REQUIRED TO BE IN THE CELL WITH YOU AND THE SUBJECT FOR THE ENTIRE INTERROGATION.

GONNA FRISK ME FOR WET PHONEBOOKS AND BLACKJACKS?

THAT WAS ABOUT AS FUNNY AS A SUCKING CHEST WOUND.

SAVE THE CLEVER STUFF FOR STORM SHADOW.

ULTRA SECURE HOLDING AREA ENTER ACCESS CODE: XXXO

HAS HE BEEN BEHAVING HIMSELF IN THERE?

BEEN QUIET AS A CHURCH MOUSE.

YEAH, WELL, IT'S EASY TO BE QUIET...

...IF YOU'RE NOT EVEN HERE!

IMPOSSIBLE!

NO WAY!

SECURITY ALERT!

LOCK DOWN THE WHOLE *PIT!*

NOT A TRACE OF THE MAN. NOT A SCRATCH ON THE DOOR OR WALLS.

SOLID ROCK ON THE OUTSIDE OF THESE WALLS! AND NO WAY HE GOT OUT THROUGH THE VENTILATION DUCT—IT'S LESS THAN A FOOT WIDE!

SO, HOW DID HE DO IT?

AWOOOGAH AWOOOGAH

MAXIMUM SECURITY ALERT! FULL LOCK-DOWN!

HE'S NOT GETTING OUT THROUGH THE ELEVATOR BANK!

NOTHING IS SHOWING UP ON THE SECURITY CAMS!

NO INFRARED ANOMALIES EITHER!

HE EVAPORATED INTO THIN AIR?

WAIT! THERE HE IS...!

...IN THE MESS HALL!

NICE TRY—BUT FUTILE...

...YOU WOULD HAVE NEVER GOTTEN PAST THE ELEVATOR BANK—

BUT I DID...

...THAT'S HOW I GOT THE REMOTE TRIGGER FOR THE PIT TO SELF-DESTRUCT. I COULD HAVE WALKED AWAY AND BLOWN ALL OF YOU UP.

SO, HOWSABOUT A LITTLE TRUST?

YOU COULD NEVER HAVE GOTTEN AWAY! GET PAST SPIRIT IRON KNIFE? NOT A CHANCE IN H—

THAT REMINDS ME...

...HE'LL BE WANTING HIS SCHMATTE BACK.

AT THE COBRA SILENT CASTLE.

AS YOU KNOW, THE PENTAGON BLOCKS SPY SATELLITES OVER UTAH AT INEXPLICABLE TIMES...

...THIS IMAGERY WAS OBTAINED IMMEDIATELY AFTER ONE OF THOSE BLACKOUTS, A MERE HALF HOUR AGO.

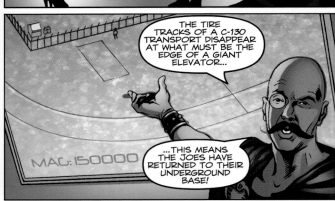

THE TIRE TRACKS OF A C-130 TRANSPORT DISAPPEAR AT WHAT MUST BE THE EDGE OF A GIANT ELEVATOR...

...THIS MEANS THE JOES HAVE RETURNED TO THEIR UNDERGROUND BASE!

MAG:150000

WHAT GOOD DOES THIS KNOWLEDGE DO US? NONE OF US CAN GET INSIDE THAT PLACE!

WE CAN'T—BUT SNAKE EYES CAN!

BRILLIANT! WE MUST IMPLEMENT THIS STRATEGY IMMEDIATELY!

FIRST WE NEED TO ESTABLISH A STAGING AREA CLOSER TO THE TARGET!

I HAVE NOTICED THAT YOUR PREVIOUS RANCOR TOWARD BILLY HAS... SOFTENED AS OF LATE, MY DEAR BARONESS.

OH? WHATEVER DO YOU MEAN, DESTRO? IS IT A NEGATIVE THING TO HAVE A MORE CIVIL RELATIONSHIP WITH THE SON OF COBRA COMMANDER?

BILLY SEEMS TO BE VERY DIFFERENT LATELY. EVEN HIS SPEECH PATTERNS AND BODY LANGUAGE HAVE ALTERED.

HE SEEMS... CRUELER.

CRUEL IS THE NEW GREED, DESTRO.

ANTONOV 24, YOU ARE CLEARED TO LAND ON RUNWAY 32L.

THANK YOU, NEWARK TOWER.

COBRA AIR TRANSPORT

GUZMAN

LUCKILY, OUR TOTAL PENETRATION OF THE CORRUPT BOROVIAN GOVERNMENT ALLOWS US TO PENETRATE THE LAUGHABLY POROUS U.S. BORDER UNDER THE AEGIS OF DIPLOMATIC IMMUNITY.

IF THE *JOES* HADN'T RAINED ON OUR PARADE, WE COULD HAVE BEEN TOTALLY IN CHARGE OF AMERICAN HOMELAND SECURITY, MINDBENDER—

WE CAN GET ALL OF THAT BACK, COBRA COMMANDER! WITH THE BRAINWASHED *SNAKE EYES* ON OUR SIDE, WE CAN PENETRATE AND DESTROY THE CORE OF THE *G.I. JOE TEAM!*

EVEN YOUR ARCANE NINJA SKILLS COULD NOT SHIELD YOUR MIND AND YOUR WILL FROM THE NEW IMPROVED BRAINWAVE SCANNER, SNAKE EYES...

...AND POOR LITTLE BILLY HAD NO CHANCE AGAINST THE GHOST THAT WAS LURKING IN THE MACHINE...

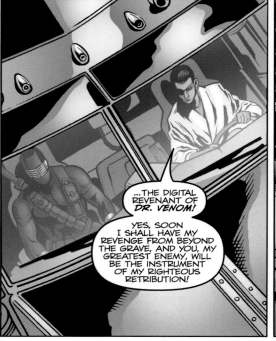

...THE DIGITAL REVENANT OF *DR. VENOM!*

YES, SOON I SHALL HAVE MY REVENGE FROM BEYOND THE GRAVE, AND YOU, MY GREATEST ENEMY, WILL BE THE INSTRUMENT OF MY RIGHTEOUS RETRIBUTION!

WHAT IS THAT BRAT NATTERING ON ABOUT TO THAT DUMB LUMP OF SCAR TISSUE? THE ENTIRE ARASHIKAGE NINJA CLAN SHOULD HAVE BEEN WIPED OFF THE FACE OF THE PLANET YEARS AGO.

ESPECIALLY *STORM SHADOW.* I HAVE A SPECIAL ARROW I'VE BEEN SAVING FOR HIM!

I'M OPENING THE FRONT RAMP—

HEY! YOU CAN'T OFFLOAD YET! TURN OFF THAT MOTOR!

V2RROOM

PULL THAT RIG OVER ON THE APRON! WE HAVE TO GET AN INSPECTOR OUT HERE!

AND WHERE'S THAT GUY ON THE MOTORCYCLE? THAT GUY WITH THE TEA TOWEL ON HIS HEAD?

I SAW HIM SCOOT OFF TOWARDS THE TAXIWAY. I'LL GO BRING HIM BACK!

UM, OKAY, TROOPER—YOU DO THAT!

POLICE

OFFICER, WE DON'T HAVE TO SUBMIT TO AN INSPECTION. THIS WHOLE RIG IS A DIPLOMATIC POUCH BY WAY OF THE BOROVIAN EMBASSY...

BROCA BROS. CIRCUS

...WE ARE PART OF A CULTURAL EXCHANGE MISSION FOR THE BETTERMENT OF INTERNATIONAL RELATIONS AND WORLD AMITY.

OH, YEAH? HOW MANY DIPLOMATIC POUCHES CONTAIN A MASKED GUY WITH A SWORD? IS HE PART OF THE CIRCUS?

HE'S OUR STAR PERFORMER, AND THERE'S THE CANNON HE GETS SHOT OUT OF.

WHAT?

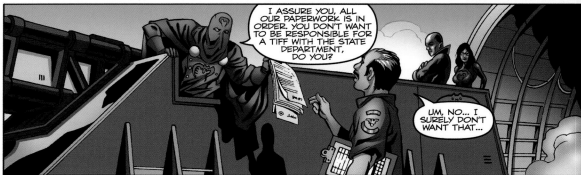

I ASSURE YOU, ALL OUR PAPERWORK IS IN ORDER. YOU DON'T WANT TO BE RESPONSIBLE FOR A TIFF WITH THE STATE DEPARTMENT, DO YOU?

UM, NO... I SURELY DON'T WANT THAT...

SHORTLY.

SOUTH 95 TRENTON ASBURY BROCA

EXIT 5

NORTH WPORT ANCASTER

ON SECOND THOUGHT, I SHOULD KNOW FROM BITTER EXPERIENCE NEVER TO UNDERESTIMATE A NINJA...

BROCA BROS. CIRCUS

...OR AN ESKIMO, FOR THAT MATTER!

I'M GOING TO HAVE TO DO A PERSONAL READJUSTMENT ON YOU VIA THE BRAINWAVE SCANNER...

...TAKE A LITTLE STROLL THROUGH THE CORRIDORS OF YOUR ID AND WREAK SOME RANDOM DESTRUCTION!

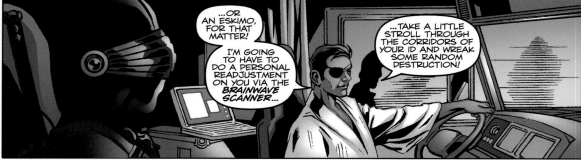

I THOUGHT ZARTAN WAS SUPPOSED TO LEAD THIS MOTORCADE.

CHANGE OF PLANS. HE WENT AHEAD TO CONTACT THE DREADNOKS...

"...IN THE PINE BARRENS."

I AM SO RAMPED! WHEN WE GET THIS *THUNDER MACHINE* BACK ON THE ROAD...

...US *DREADNOKS* GONNA BE *UNSTOPPABLE!*

I'M GETTING A BIT PECKISH, I AM! GETTING CLOSE TO HAVING A LOW-SUGAR INCIDENT!

THAT'S A SCOOT OUTSIDE...

...SOMEBODY'S PULLING UP IN FRONT. SOUNDS LIKE A PAN-HEAD...

...ULP! ELECTRAGLIDE IN BLUE!

OKAY, EVERYBODY GET READY—

—GET HIM! OFF THE PIG!

YEE-HA!

I KNEW *THRASHER* WAS IGNORANT...

WHAPP

WHOMP

...BUT I EXPECTED SOME MINIMAL COMPETENCY FROM YOU, *RIPPER!*

BUZZER, YOU WERE ALWAYS A PROBLEM CHILD!

THWAMM

AND *TORCH,* YOU ARE IN PERPETUAL NEED OF *UPLIFT!*

SPLOOT

NOW, HAVE YOUR FEEBLE BRAINS FIGURED OUT WHAT'S GOING ON YET, OR DO I HAVE TO DO A POWERPOINT PRESENTATION?

THOOM

PATHETIC...

HOW'D THIS PIG KNOW OUR NAMES?

OWW.

...SIMPLY PATHETIC.

ZARTAN! HOW WERE WE SUPPOSED TO KNOW IT WAS *YOU?*

AND ANYWAY, WE'VE BEEN WAITING HERE SO LONG WITHOUT ANY FOOD THAT I'M BEGINNING TO GET THAT HYPOGLYCEMIC CRANKINESS!

BUZZER'S HARD TO TAKE WHEN HE'S CRANKY!

HE'S HARD TO TAKE WHEN HE'S NOT!

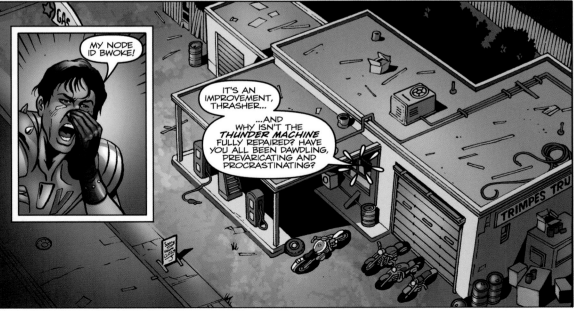

MY NODE ID BWOKE!

IT'S AN IMPROVEMENT, THRASHER...

...AND WHY ISN'T THE *THUNDER MACHINE* FULLY REPAIRED? HAVE YOU ALL BEEN DAWDLING, PREVARICATING AND PROCRASTINATING?

HEY, WE'RE *UPGRADING* AS WE GO! BETTER ARMOR! OVERDRIVE! *ABS* BRAKES!

I JUST WANT IT UP AND RUNNING...

...THERE ARE SOME BIG SHAKE-UPS COMING IN THE COBRA COMMAND STRUCTURE, AND I WANT TO BE ABLE TO EXPLOIT EVERY OPPORTUNITY TO FEATHER OUR OWN NEST.

WELL, THESE LITTLE CHICKADEES AIN'T BEEN *FED*...

...AND THIS PARTICULAR NESTLING AIN'T DOING *JACK* UNTIL HE GETS SOME CARBS AND SUGAR! YOU SHOULD TAKE US ALL OUT, OR ORDER IN!

WE'RE SUPPOSED TO BE KEEPING A LOW PROFILE HERE! WHAT WE'RE DOING IS SUPPOSED TO BE A *SECRET*!

SOMEBODY HAD BETTER BRING US SOME FOOD AND DRINK, OR ELSE *NOTHING* IS GONNA GET DONE.

IN THE TOWN OF BROCA BEACH, ON THE JERSEY SHORE.

...THEY WANT *WHAT?*

CHOCOLATE-COVERED DONUTS AND GRAPE SODA?!

I'M IN THE MIDDLE OF SOMETHING, ZARTAN...

...I'LL DEAL WITH IT WHEN I CAN!

WELCOME COMM

DESTRO! WHAT ARE ALL THESE PEOPLE DOING OUT HERE WITH BANNERS AND A MARCHING BAND?

THEY'VE IMPROVISED A LITTLE WELCOME, COMMANDER.

THIS WELCOME IS DECIDEDLY *UNWELCOME!* OUR ARRIVAL WAS SUPPOSED TO BE *SUB ROSA!* DISPERSE THIS RABBLE!

LEAVE IT TO ME, COBRA COMMANDER.

I HATE BALLOONS!

THE COMMANDER EXTENDS HIS HEARTFELT GRATITUDE FOR THIS SPONTANEOUS DISPLAY OF AFFECTION, BUT WISHES EVERYBODY TO PLEASE RETURN TO BUSINESS AS USUAL...

MAKE SURE ALL THE VEHICLES ARE SECURED INSIDE THE WAX MUSEUM. I DON'T WANT ANY OF THEM SHOWING UP ON SATELLITE PHOTOS.

ANYBODY WEARING A COBRA UNIFORM SHOULD REMAIN INSIDE AS WELL.

YOU *VIPERS* BE CAREFUL! THAT'S A VERY DELICATE PIECE OF TECHNOLOGY YOU'RE UNLOADING!

THE BRAINWAVE SCANNER IS ABOUT AS DELICATE AS AN ELECTRIC CHAIR!

IF YOU DON'T WATCH YOUR MOUTH YOU MIGHT BE SITTING IN IT YOURSELF!

YES, IF ANY OF YOU DOLTS DAMAGES MY SCANNER, HEADS WILL ROLL!

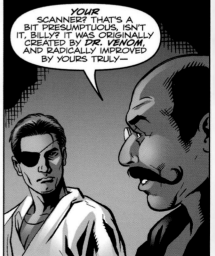

YOUR SCANNER? THAT'S A BIT PRESUMPTUOUS, ISN'T IT, BILLY? IT WAS ORIGINALLY CREATED BY *DR. VENOM*, AND RADICALLY IMPROVED BY YOURS TRULY—

IMPROVED? YOU CAN'T IMPROVE ON WHAT WAS ORIGINALLY A PERFECT WORK OF GENIUS!

AND I'M NOT PRESUMPTUOUS, I'M *RIGHT!*

DON'T YOU AGREE, SNAKE EYES?

SAY, WHAT DO YOU SAY WE PLOP YOU INTO THE CHAIR AND GIVE YOU AN EXTRA ZAP JUST TO KEEP YOUR NEURONS JUMPING?

WHY, IT WILL BE JUST LOADS OF FUN! *STIMULATING*, TOO—

—DESTRO! WHY ARE YOU STARING AT ME LIKE THAT?

STOP IT RIGHT THIS INSTANT! JUST WHO DO YOU THINK YOU ARE?

I KNOW WHO I AM.

DO YOU KNOW WHO YOU ARE?

EXCUSE ME.

I NEED TO GET SOME AIR.

NOW ON DISPLAY

CU T RDS AST STAND

NONE OF US SHOULD BE OUT HERE UNLESS WE ARE IN MUFTI, BARONESS.

I WAS CHECKING SECURITY...

BROCA B
WAX MU

NOW ON DISPLAY

CU T RDS AST STAND

...AND I DON'T THINK THAT SURFER COUPLE OUT THERE LOOK LIKE "LOCALS."

BROCA
WAX MUSEUM

SHOOTING GALLERY

AH, THERE YOU ARE, BARONESS!

I REQUIRE YOU TO UNDERTAKE AN EXTREMELY IMPORTANT MISSION!

STORM SHADOW'S TIP WAS RIGHT ON THE MONEY, TORPEDO! JUST LOOK AT THAT LINEUP ON THE BOARDWALK!

IT MAKES A LOT OF SENSE, LADY JAYE...

...COBRA USING BROCA BEACH AS A STAGING AREA MAKES LOGISTICS MANAGEABLE.

THIS PLACE IS LIKE THE JERSEY SHORE EQUIVALENT OF SPRINGFIELD.

WELL! SHE CERTAINLY WENT OFF IN A HUFF!

THAT "MISSION" YOU GAVE HER WAS MORE LIKE AN ERRAND, COMMANDER.

WISH I COULD HAVE BEEN A FLY ON THE WALL DURING THE CONVERSATION THAT SPARKED THAT REACTION FROM THE BARONESS!

I THINK SHE'S UP TO SOMETHING. WE HAVE TO BE PREPARED TO FOLLOW HER.

...AND YOU WILL RECOGNIZE THIS, OF COURSE, AS THE *BATTLE OF COBRA ISLAND*...

...IT PORTRAYS THE EVENT RATHER ACCURATELY, IF I DO SAY SO MYSELF.

BATTLE OF COBRA ISLAND

THE EDITORIAL DIRECTION SEEMS TO FAVOR *COBRA*.

THE ONLY PEOPLE WHO EVER SAW IT WERE THE GOOD CITIZENS OF BROCA BEACH WHO ARE ALL LOYAL COBRAS. WE SHOW THEM WHAT THEY WANT TO SEE.

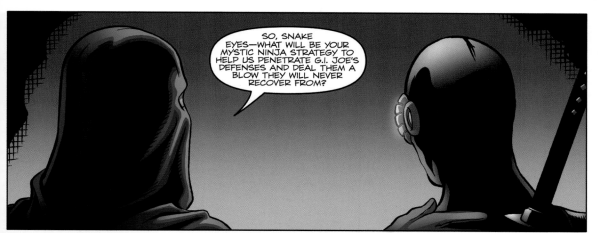

SO, SNAKE EYES—WHAT WILL BE YOUR MYSTIC NINJA STRATEGY TO HELP US PENETRATE G.I. JOE'S DEFENSES AND DEAL THEM A BLOW THEY WILL NEVER RECOVER FROM?

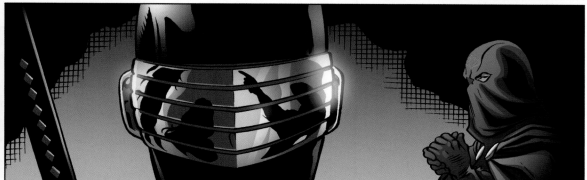

ZZZAASSSSH

THWITIIIPP

THUMP

NEAR THE PINE BARRENS.

THAT'S THE SECOND CARTLOAD OF GRAPE SODA AND CHOCOLATE-COVERED DONUTS SHE'S HAULED OUT TO HER CAR...

...WE CAN MAKE A SAFE GUESS AS TO WHAT DERANGED BIKER COHORTS OF ZARTAN THOSE ARE INTENDED FOR.

AND WHAT A NERVE...

...WEARING HER WHOLE BLACK LEATHER OUTFIT OUT IN THE OPEN LIKE THAT!

IT IS THE JERSEY SHORE, YOU KNOW!

IF SHE TAKES OFF IN ANY DIRECTION OTHER THAN BACK TO BROCA BEACH, WE KNOW SHE IS HOOKING UP WITH THE DREADNOKS.

THERE SHE GOES! SHE'S HEADING INLAND!

LET'S GO!

HMMMMM...

HANG BACK A BIT, TORPEDO. WE DON'T WANT HER TO SUSS OUR TAIL JOB.

WHAT? WHERE'D THAT CRAZY *WAHINE* GO?

LOOK OUT! SHE WAS HIDING BEHIND THE *BILLBOARD!*

WHAMMO

SKREEEE

KA-SHOOMP

AND NOW FOR *LES COUPS DE GRACE!*

WHAT'S THIS? WHERE'S THE OTHER ONE?

RIGHT BEHIND YOU, BARONESS!

YOU'LL HAVE TO DO BETTER THAN THAT TO TAKE *ME* DOWN!

THWUMP

I'VE BEEN TRAINING HARD LATELY— —SPARRING WITH A BONA-FIDE *NINJA!*

WHAPP

WHAPP

THOOM

HOW CAN YOU WITHSTAND THIS? WHY DON'T YOU FALL DOWN?

44

TORPEDO! ARE YOU ALL RIGHT?

FEEL LIKE I WIPED OUT IN A BIG PIPE, BUT OTHER THAN THAT...

...I SEE YOU'VE BEEN BUSY, GIRL.

JUST A BIT. LET'S WINCH THE *VAMP* BACK ONTO THE ROAD AND GET THIS PIECE OF TRASH BACK TO WHERE PSYCHE-OUT CAN WORK HIS MAGIC ON HER.

LATER.

SO WHERE IS THAT SOW WITH OUR GRUB?

I'M ABOUT TO KEEL OVER FROM BERI-BERI!

IT'S AN ANOMALY THAT PORTENDS ILL.

PACK UP AND STERILIZE THE PREMISES...

...WE'VE BEEN COMPROMISED.

46

DEEP BELOW THE UTAH DESERT, IN THE PIT.

"THE BARONESS IS NOT A HAPPY CAMPER TODAY..."

...BUT THEN AGAIN, I CAN'T SAY I'VE SEEN HER IN A GOOD MOOD.

IT STRIKES ME AS BAD ACTING, STALKER. SHE'S THROWING A FIT TO COVER UP SOMETHING ELSE.

I AGREE, DUKE. IT'S A BLIND OR A DIVERSION. ANY ANOMALIES ON INFRARED OR AUDIO SCANS, MAINFRAME?

ZILCH. ALL CLEAN.

SHE'S IN THE SAME CELL YOU WERE IN, STORM SHADOW—SAY, HOW DID YOU GET OUT OF IT, ANYWAY?

NO FAULT ON G.I. JOE SECURITY OR THE STRUCTURAL INTEGRITY OF THE CELL. IT JUST WASN'T DESIGNED TO HOLD A NINJA. I DOUBT THAT BARONESS CAN MANAGE TO GET OUT OF IT ON HER OWN.

...AND HERE'S SOMETHING FOR YOU VOYEURISTIC CREEPS!

48

THAT SURVEILLANCE CAM SHOULD HAVE BEEN ARMORED!

THE MICROPHONE WAS PART OF THAT CAMERA RIG!

IT WILL TAKE AT LEAST THREE MINUTES TO OPEN THAT HIGH-SECURITY CELL DOOR AND REPLACE THOSE MONITORING DEVICES!

SHE CAN GET INTO AN AWFUL LOT OF MISCHIEF IN THREE MINUTES.

THAT'S AN UNDERSTATEMENT!

I'M CALLING A FULL SECURITY ALERT AND TOTAL LOCK-DOWN!

LOCK-DOWN COUNTING DOWN, DUKE! THE PIT WILL BE SEALED IN 30 SECONDS!

STORM SHADOW, WE NEED YOU TO—

—WHU? WHERE DID HE DISAPPEAR TO?

I HATE WHEN HE DOES THAT. HE FALLS RIGHT OFF THE SENSOR FIELDS.

IN BROCA BEACH,
ON THE JERSEY DRIVE.

...NOT ANOTHER TIRING TIRADE, PLEASE, DESTRO.

IT HAS BEEN A WEEK SINCE THE DISAPPEARANCE OF THE BARONESS, COBRA COMMANDER! WHY HASN'T ANYTHING BEEN DONE?

YOU'RE NOT CONSIDERING THE BIG PICTURE. BARONESS IS JUST A SMALL COG IN A VAST MACHINE.

WE CAN'T STOP THE JUGGERNAUT FOR ONE INDIVIDUAL, CAN WE?

CAN WE, DESTRO? HMMMM?

THE JOES DON'T THINK THAT WAY.

THEN WHY DID THEY ABANDON SNAKE EYES TO HIS FATE?

I'M HAVING MISGIVINGS, BILLY...

ABOUT WHAT, DR. MINDBENDER?

...UM... PERHAPS YOU SHOULDN'T BE HAVING SO MANY SESSIONS IN THE BRAINWAVE SCANNER...

WHY? IS THERE SOMETHING WRONG WITH IT?

BASEMENT
NO ADMITTANCE
AUTHORIZED STA
ONLY
ALARM WILL SOUND

OF COURSE NOT! ER... IT'S WORKING EVEN BETTER THAN IT EVER DID!

THEN THERE'S NO PROBLEM WITH CONTINUING TO USE IT.

I FIND IT... INVIGORATING.

SCANNER ONLINE

51

MAYBE THAT'S SOMETHING TO BE CONCERNED ABOUT. *NOBODY* SHOULD WANT TO SUBMIT TO A SCANNER SESSION!

PERHAPS ITS POTENCY HAS BEEN DEGRADED—

NONSENSE. I CAN ASSURE YOU THAT THE SESSIONS ARE JUST AS EXCRUCIATING AS THEY HAVE EVER BEEN. "NO PAIN, NO GAIN," AS THE SAYING GOES.

AND IF THE SCANNER ISN'T AS EFFICIENT AS IT USED TO BE, WOULDN'T THAT THROW THE NEW PRO-COBRA STATUS OF SNAKE EYES INTO CONTENTION?

YOU *DID* ASSURE MY FATHER THAT THE CONVERSION WAS BEYOND REFUTE, AS I RECALL.

I... I MAY HAVE MADE THAT ASSERTION...

THEN, WHAT IS THERE TO TALK ABOUT? HIT THE SWITCH, WILL YOU?

SCANNER

HOOOOO HAAAAAA...

ENGAGE SCANNER
PROGRAM SERIES
ACTION
ACTIVATE
?

IN UTAH.

CLUNK

CLUNK
CLUNK

BWWAA!

THAT PIPE WAS NARROWER THAN I EXPECTED...

...SHOULD INCLUDE RIBCAGE COMPRESSION IN MY DAILY TRAINING.

WHUMP

HOLD IT RIGHT THERE, STORM SHADOW...

...I THOUGHT YOU MIGHT MAKE A RUN FOR IT. NEAT TRICK WITH THE WATER PIPE

NOTHING THAT HOUDINI COULDN'T PULL OFF. I'M NOT RUNNING AWAY, YOU KNOW...

...I'M GOING AFTER MY—SWORD BROTHER.

YOU FIND HIM, AND YOU NEED HELP ON THE EXTRACTION, YOU CALL ME. YOU UNDERSTAND?

WHUMP

YOU'LL NEED REAL CLOTHES. THERE'S SOME CASH, AS WELL. WE PASSED THE HAT AROUND.

I... I UNDERESTIMATED BOTH OF YOU... I'M...

HE'LL BRING HIM BACK, SCARLETT.

OR DIE TRYING.

IN BROCA BEACH.

HA HA! THAT WAS EXHAUSTINGLY INSTAURATIONAL!

REALLY? THERE WAS STEAM ISSUING FROM YOUR EARS.

I AM BEGINNING TO FEEL MORE LIKE MYSELF WITH EVERY SESSION.

YOU *SOUND* LESS AND LESS LIKE YOURSELF...

...YOU'RE BEGINNING TO SOUND LIKE DR. VENOM!

I'LL TAKE THAT AS A COMPLIMENT.

IF YOU WISH...

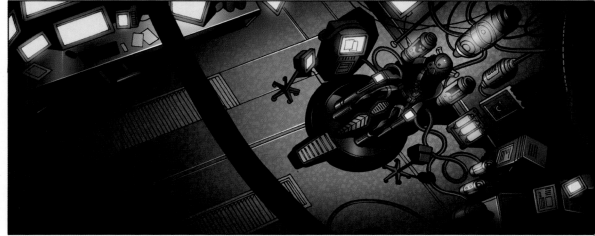

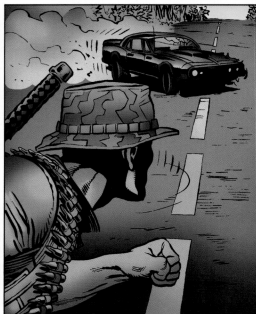

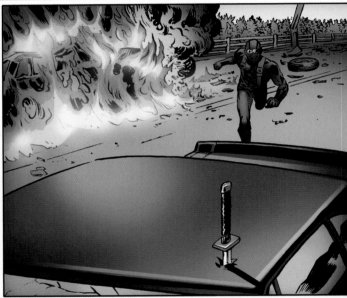

IN NEW JERSEY.

THIS IS WHERE IT ALL WENT DOWN, DESTRO.

IT LOOKS LIKE SHE WAS BEHIND THE BILLBOARD, AND THAT SHE RAMMED THE G.I. JOE *VAMP*...

...FORCING IT OFF THE ROAD INTO THE CRANBERRY BOG.

YOU DIDN'T BOTHER TO DRAG THE BOG, DID YOU, ZARTAN?

SPLOOT

...OR YOU MIGHT HAVE FOUND *THIS*.

IT DOESN'T HELP TO KNOW THIS, SINCE WE DON'T KNOW WHERE THE JOES ARE...

DON'T WE?

TELE-VIPER, LET US HAVE THAT HOLOGRAPHIC DISPLAY, PLEASE.

COMING RIGHT UP, DESTRO.

WE HAVE LONG SUSPECTED THAT THE JOES HAVE A VAST UNDERGROUND BASE HIDDEN UNDER THIS TINY BASE IN UTAH...

I'VE BEEN INSIDE THEIR OLD UNDERGROUND BASE IN STATEN ISLAND. A MORE RECENT BASE WOULD HAVE DEFENSES AND HARDENING THAT ARE OVER THE TOP. COBRA, IN ITS PRESENT STATE, COULD NEVER PENETRATE—

A FRONTAL ASSAULT WOULD FAIL. BUT A SMALL UNIT LED BY AN UNNAMED INDIVIDUAL WHO CAN IMPERSONATE ONE OF THE JOES MIGHT STAND A CHANCE.

IF ZARTAN IS IN, SO AM I!

ME TOO!

CAN WE TALK ABOUT THIS FIRST?

IN THE PIT.

HIS NEW SURVEILLANCE UNIT IS BUILT TO WITHSTAND A GRENADE. SHE'S NOT GOING TO DISABLE IT.

WE'VE SEARCHED AND SCANNED EVERY SQUARE INCH OF THIS SHELL AND THERE'S NOTHING AMISS...

...BUT THE BARONESS *MUST* HAVE SHUT DOWN THE CAM FOR A REASON!

WE KNOW SHE IS CAPABLE OF CONVOLUTED THINKING. *WHY* WOULD SHE DRAW ATTENTION TO SOMETHING LIKE THAT? WHAT DOES SHE *GAIN*?

SHE'S TESTING OUR RESPONSE. PROBING FOR WEAK SPOTS.

HA! I DON'T HAVE TO DIG DEEP TO FIND ANY OF *THOSE!*

IT MAY NOT HAVE BEEN THE GREATEST MOVE IN THE WORLD TO BRING THE BARONESS DOWN HERE INTO THE PIT.

JUST WHERE DO WE STAND ON THIS LEGALLY?

SHE ATTACKED LADY JAYE AND TORPEDO WITH INTENT TO DO BODILY HARM. SHE ALSO DAMAGED GOVERNMENT PROPERTY...

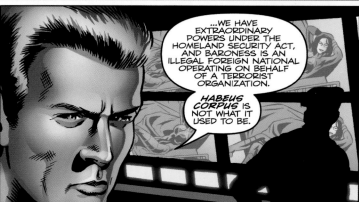

...WE HAVE EXTRAORDINARY POWERS UNDER THE HOMELAND SECURITY ACT, AND BARONESS IS AN ILLEGAL FOREIGN NATIONAL OPERATING ON BEHALF OF A TERRORIST ORGANIZATION.

HABEUS CORPUS IS NOT WHAT IT USED TO BE.

WE HAVE TO DOUBLE OUR PERIMETER O.P.s*, STALKER...

*OBSERVATION POSTS.

PUT SPIRIT IRON KNIFE IN CHARGE OF A ROVING PATROL TO COVER THE AREAS BEYOND THE O.P.s.

STP 23

GULF

PENNEZN

HOW ABOUT PLANS FOR GETTING SNAKE EYES BACK?

STORM SHADOW IS ON THAT. HOW MUCH MORE CAN WE RAIN ON COBRA'S PARADE?

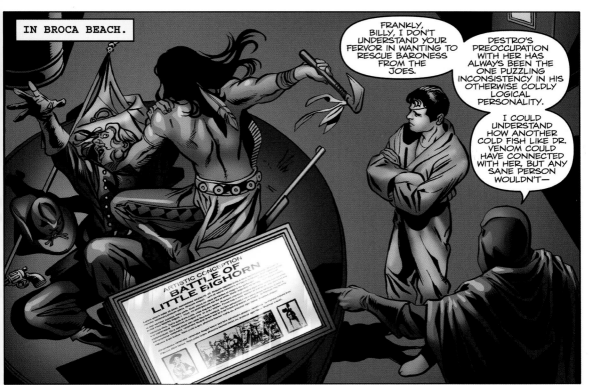

IN BROCA BEACH.

FRANKLY, BILLY, I DON'T UNDERSTAND YOUR FERVOR IN WANTING TO RESCUE BARONESS FROM THE JOES.

DESTRO'S PREOCCUPATION WITH HER HAS ALWAYS BEEN THE ONE PUZZLING INCONSISTENCY IN HIS OTHERWISE COLDLY LOGICAL PERSONALITY.

I COULD UNDERSTAND HOW ANOTHER COLD FISH LIKE DR. VENOM COULD HAVE CONNECTED WITH HER, BUT ANY SANE PERSON WOULDN'T—

DR. VENOM IS—WAS—A GENIUS! AND WE CAN'T AFFORD TO HAVE THE JOES PRY ALL THE NASTY LITTLE SECRETS OUT OF THE BARONESS' BRAIN, CAN WE?

NNNNNGGHH!

OKAY, WE'LL GET HER BACK! YOU DON'T HAVE TO CARRY ON LIKE—

THE SCANNER! SOMEONE'S USING THE SCANNER!

SNAKE EYES!

HE'S GOT THE ADMINISTRATOR'S KEY!

ATTENTION BRAINWAVE SCANNER

NO ADMITTANCE

HE CAN GET INTO THE SCANNER'S SYSTEM—

—NOOOOOOO!

NOOOOOO!

IN THE BASEMENT OF THE WAX MUSEUM IN BROCA BEACH.

WHA—! SNAKE EYES HAS BYPASSED THE INTERNAL SECURITY AND ENTERED THE SHARED-CONSCIOUSNESS CONTROL SECTOR OF THE BRAINWAVE SCANNER!

PROGRAM ACTIVE!

YOU WISH TO OVERRIDE

IF HE CONFRONTS DR. VENOM IN THERE, THE RESULTS COULD BE DISASTROUS!

THERE'S NO WAY WE CAN LET THAT HAPPEN! HAVE TO SWAP AVATARS IN THERE...

...AND DEAL WITH IT!

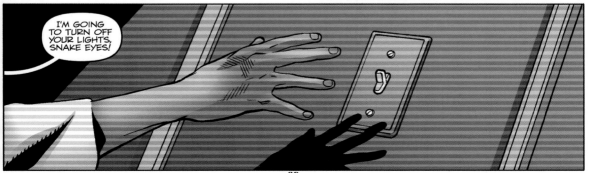

I'M GOING TO TURN OFF YOUR LIGHTS, SNAKE EYES!

BUT YOU SHOULD KNOW WHO YOU ARE REALLY UP AGAINST.

YES, *DR. VENOM* LIVES ON DIGITALLY! ISN'T SCIENCE WONDERFUL?

I KNEW YOU'D BE SPEECHLESS.

CLICK

THAT WAS... DRAINING.

YES, WHAT DO YOU WANT, DR. MINDBENDER?

WE INTERCEPTED SOME SATELLITE IMAGERY THAT INDICATES STORM SHADOW MAY HAVE LEFT THE SUSPECTED G.I. JOE FACILITY IN UTAH.

LATER.

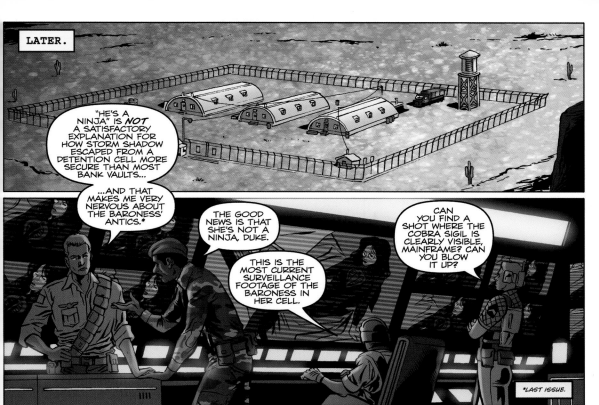

"HE'S A NINJA" IS *NOT* A SATISFACTORY EXPLANATION FOR HOW STORM SHADOW ESCAPED FROM A DETENTION CELL MORE SECURE THAN MOST BANK VAULTS...

...AND THAT MAKES ME VERY NERVOUS ABOUT THE BARONESS' ANTICS.*

THE GOOD NEWS IS THAT SHE'S NOT A NINJA, DUKE.

THIS IS THE MOST CURRENT SURVEILLANCE FOOTAGE OF THE BARONESS IN HER CELL.

CAN YOU FIND A SHOT WHERE THE COBRA SIGIL IS CLEARLY VISIBLE, MAINFRAME? CAN YOU BLOW IT UP?

*LAST ISSUE.

IS THIS BIG ENOUGH?

FIND ANYTHING, PSYCHE-OUT?

IT'S WHAT I *DIDN'T* FIND, DUKE. THIRD BAR DOWN ON THE LEFT IN THE SIGIL. IT'S MISSING.

LET'S SEE WHAT THAT SIGIL LOOKED LIKE *BEFORE* SHE TRASHED THE CAM IN HER CELL AND WE HAD TO GO IN THERE AND REPLACE IT...

...IT WAS *THERE!*

SO WHAT HAPPENED TO IT?

WE SEARCHED THE CELL THOROUGHLY WHEN WE SWITCHED CAMS. IT DEFINITELY WAS NOT THERE.

WHAT WAS THAT THING, ANYWAY?

WITH NANO-TECHNOLOGY, IT COULD HAVE BEEN ANYTHING!

STALKER, WE HAVE TO DOUBLE THE NUMBER OF JOES ASSIGNED TO SPIRIT IRON KNIFE'S OUTER PERIMETER PATROLS. GET SNEAK-PEEK OUT THERE.

OH, AND TELL HARDTOP AND CROSS-COUNTRY TO EXECUTE THE *GREER SHIFT* TO "LOCUS B."

I'M ON IT, DUKE.

HAVE THE SCANNERS PICKED UP ANY ANOMALIES *OUTSIDE* BARONESS' CELL?

NADA, ZIP, ZERO. YOU THINK THAT WAS HER INTENT...

...TO GET *US* TO GO INTO HER CELL SO SHE COULD GET SOMETHING *OUT?*

BUT FOR WHAT REASON? OR IS IT ALL JUST A DIVERSION? I WISH I COULD FATHOM HOW HER MIND WORKS!

IN BROCA BEACH.

YOU'RE NOT WINDED ALREADY, ARE YOU, TELE-VIPER?

NO, COBRA COMMANDER, SIR! I'M... -:PANT PANT:- FINE.

EXCELLENT! THEN YOU CAN GIVE ME AN UPDATE ON ALL OUR ONGOING COBRA OPERATIONS!

I'M PATCHING THROUGH A VIDEO LINK FROM DR. MINDBENDER ON THE C-PHONE.

I HOPE THAT SHINY-PATED TWIT HAS SOME GOOD NEWS FOR A CHANGE...

WE ARE APPROACHING THE SITE OF THE SUSPECTED JOE BASE IN UTAH...

...BUT WE HAVE HAD NO CONTACT WITH DESTRO OR ZARTAN, WHO ARE SUPPOSED TO BE SETTING UP A DIVERSION FOR OUR ATTACK.

THERE IS COMPLETE SILENCE ON THE SECURE CHANNEL, AND I AM AFRAID WE MIGHT ALERT THE JOES IF WE ATTEMPT OTHER MEANS OF COMMUNICATION—

YOU DON'T NEED A DIVERSION! YOU HAVE THE DISTINCT ADVANTAGE OF COMPLETE SURPRISE!

INITIATE THE ASSAULT AS SOON AS YOU ARE IN POSITION! NO MORE OF THIS SHILLY-SHALLYING AROUND!

LET US PROCEED, SHALL WE, TELE-VIPER?

PREPARE TO DEPLOY THE B.A.T.S!*

*BATTLE ANDROID TROOPERS

"...SET THEM ON 'NO PRISONERS,' AND CRANK THE 'RUN AMOK' DIAL UP TO 10.

"DID YOU REMEMBER TO ACTIVATE THE RANDOM DELAY PROXIMITY FUSES AND ARM THEIR SATCHEL CHARGES?"

"THEY ARE GOOD TO GO, DR. MINDBENDER."

THAT'S ODD. THE B.A.T.S ARE HEADING PRECISELY TOWARD WHERE THE G.I. JOE BASE IS SUPPOSED TO BE, BUT THERE'S NOTHING THERE—

THERE'S A SMALL MILITARY BASE OFF TO THE LEFT...

THAT'S IT! THE GPS MUST BE WONKY! REDIRECT THE B.A.T.S VISUALLY!

FIVE KILOMETERS AWAY.

THE B.A.T.S JUST VEERED OFF COURSE. THEY'RE HEADING FOR THAT LITTLE BASE TWO AND HALF KILOMETERS AWAY BY MY RANGE FINDER.

THAT'S WHACK, ZARTAN. ACCORDING TO THE DATA WE GOT FROM THE SATELLITE, *WE'RE* STANDING RIGHT ON TOP OF THE G.I. JOE BASE...

...BUT THERE'S NOTHING HERE BUT SAND AND CACTI!

WHAT'S A CACK-TIE?

YOU *ARE* IN THE CORRECT LOCATION! THE SURFACE BASE HAS BEEN *MOVED!*

THE SECRET FACILITY IN QUESTION IS *BELOW* THE SAND...

WHOA! CHECK IT OUT! UM... WHAT *IS* IT?

IT'S THE OTHER HALF OF A FAST UNCOUPLING CONNECTION. IT LOOKS LIKE IT USED TO BE HOOKED UP TO A WATER TOWER...

RUN AMOK! RUN AMOK!

MAIM! MANGLE! MUTILATE!

NO PRISONERS! NO PRISONERS!

REPORT: NO HUMAN TARGETS ON SITE. SCANNING FOR UNDERGROUND ANOMALIES.

THERE'S NOTHING UNDER THOSE BUILDINGS BUT SAND AND ROCK. ECHO SOUNDINGS REVEAL NO HIDDEN BASE!

IT *HAS* TO BE THERE! THEY COULDN'T JUST MOVE THE WHOLE BASE! COULD THEY?

TA-DAA!

GOOD JOB, TORCH!

TIME TO KNOCK SOME HEADS, EH, ZARTAN?

IT WOULD BE STUPID TO ASSUME THAT THE JOES DON'T KNOW WE ARE HERE. WE ARE *NOT* GOING TO SURPRISE THEM AT ALL...

...WHAT WE *CAN* DO...

...IS TO SOW A MODICUM OF CONFUSION.

SOUND DAMPERS AND INFRARED CLOAKING *ON.*

THIS IS SO *COOL—*

SHUT UP, THRASHER.

DESTRO JUST COMPROMISED THE SURVEILLANCE CAMS AND HE'S GOT SOMETHING SPOOFING THE HEAT SENSORS AND MICS AS WELL!

NG TO THE MAX.

REPROGRAM THE *B.A.T.S* TO ATTACK THE CORRECT *GPS* COORDINATES!

DESTRO, ZARTAN AND THE DREADNOKS HAVE DISAPPEARED INTO A DUST CLOUD!

AND THE B.A.T.S ARE NOW HEADING FOR THE ACTUAL *PIT LOCATION.* IS IT TIME TO FLIP OVER THE HOLE CARDS, SERGEANT IRON KNIFE?

ALMOST THERE, SNEAK-PEEK. GIVE ME A MINUTE TO GO OVER AND DEAL WITH THE BAD GUYS IN THE DUST...

...AND THEN LIGHT UP THE B.A.T.S WITH THE LASER DESIGNATOR AND GIVE ACE THE GREEN LIGHT TO PICKLE TWO PAVEWAYS.

ROGER THAT!

MEANWHILE, IN THE SECURITY DETENTION CELL OF THE PIT.

TESTING, ONE TWO THREE...

LASER DESIGNATOR ON AND LOCKED...

"...IS THAT SIGNAL HOT ENOUGH FOR YOU, ACE?"

I HAVE A SOLID LOCK TONE, SNEAK-PEEK...

...ORDNANCE AWAY!

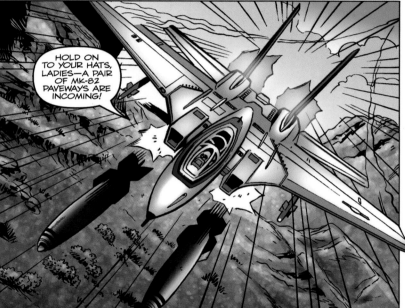

HOLD ON TO YOUR HATS, LADIES—A PAIR OF MK-82 PAVEWAYS ARE INCOMING!

TAKE COVER! TAKE COVER!

YOWP!

WHOOMP

BRRRINGGG

IT'S FOR YOU, DR. MINDBENDER...

URK!

BRRRINGGG

HOW'S THE ATTACK PROGRESSING? I HOPE YOU ARE UTILIZING THE B.A.T.S JUDICIOUSLY...

...THAT NEW MODEL IS SETTING US BACK A COOL MIL-POINT-FIVE A PIECE—

—SPEAK UP! IT SOUNDS LIKE IT'S RAINING SCRAP METAL OVER THERE! HOLD ON, I HAVE A MESSAGE COMING IN FROM BILLY—

SNAKE EYES AND I ARE APPROACHING NEW YORK CITY...

...I KNOW THE LOCATION OF STORM SHADOW'S SECRET LAIR IN MANHATTAN AND WE ARE GOING TO SET UP A LITTLE SURPRISE FOR HIM THERE!

CLASS 3 JAMMER! SOMEBODY IS TRYING TO SHUT DOWN ALL OUR SCANNERS AND SURVEILLANCE ON THE ENTRANCE SHAFTS!

IT'S INTERMITTENT. WHY IS THAT?

ENCRYPTED BURST TRANSMISSIONS. SOMEBODY IS TRYING TO COMMUNICATE INTERNALLY FROM THE *PIT!*

I THINK I JUST FOUND THAT MISSING BAR FROM THE BARONESS' COBRA SIGIL...

...STUCK TO THE BACK OF MAINFRAME'S HELMET!

IT'S NOT A SIMPLE TRANSCEIVER. IT'S A SCANNER, A BOOSTER AND A RELAY. IT'S BEEN RUNNING A SEARCH ON OUR DATABASE AND FORWARDING THE INFO—

THE *BARONESS!*

DESTRO AND ZARTAN NOW KNOW WHERE SHE IS BEING HELD AND THEY ARE GOING TO SPRING HER!

THAT'S IT! THAT *WATER TANK!* THAT'S STORM SHADOW'S SECRET LAIR!

I SEE! YOU WANT A SAFE PERCH TO OBSERVE THE WATER TANK BEFORE WE MAKE AN ASSAULT ON IT...

NO PARKING 6:00 AM TO 6:00 P

...HOLD IT STEADY AND HOVER, GYRO-VIPER!

SNAKE EYES! I *KNEW* YOU WOULD DO A RECON BEFORE YOU ATTACKED MY HIDEOUT, AND THIS IS THE PERFECT SPOT FOR IT!

WE HAVE A LOT TO SETTLE, SWORD-BROTHER...

...BUT FIRST, LET'S NULLIFY THE INTERFERENCE!

WE DO PREFER A LEVEL PLAYING FIELD FOR THESE CONTESTS OF SKILL, DO WE NOT?

SPONK

AN OBVIOUS OPENING ATTACK—BUT YOU'RE JUST TESTING THE WATERS, AREN'T YOU?

KTANG

TAIL ROTOR'S OUT! GYRO-VIPER—

—KILL THE ENGINES AND AUTO-ROTATE!

SETTING UP A DŌ-THRUST, HUH? OH, BY THE WAY...

...WATCH OUT BEHIND YOU!

THWAMM

I HAVE TO ADMIT, I MISJUDGED THAT ONE A BIT...

...BUT I SEE THAT YOUR DEFENSE IS JUST AS GOOD AS EVER!

IN THE PIT.

SPIRIT IRON KNIFE IS TOPSIDE WITH FIVE PRISONERS...

...AND ONE OF THEM IS THE *BARONESS!*

THAT CAN'T *BE*...

...*SECURITY SECTION!* GET THE DETENTION CELLS BACK ON LINE AND CHECK ON THE *BARONESS!*

THE CAM IS BACK UP, BUT BARONESS IS *NOT* IN HER CELL!

NO WAY SHE DID A HOUDINI! I TELL YOU, SHE'S *IN* THERE, STALKER!

WHAT'S THAT *WHOOSHING* SOUND—?

ONLY ONE WAY TO FIND OUT, ROADBLOCK—

HEADS UP! IT'S *DESTRO!*

TAKE COVER BEHIND THE CELL DOOR...

FOOOSH

TIME TO DEPART, MY DEAR BARONESS!

FOOOSH

...BEFORE WE GET NAILED BY HIS *WRIST ROCKETS!*

IT'S ABOUT TIME, DESTRO!

HOW DID SHE MANAGE TO BE IN TWO PLACES AT THE SAME TIME?

WELL, TECHNICALLY, SHE'S NO LONGER IN *THIS* PLACE!

AND I THINK I JUST REALIZED *WHO* IT REALLY IS THAT SPIRIT IRON KNIFE HAS PRISONER UPSTAIRS!

LOOK OUT!

SOME B.A.T.S SURVIVED THE BOMBING! THOSE THINGS ARE JUST WALKING TIME BOMBS PACKED WITH SEMTEX!

SEMTEX IS STABLE. BULLET IMPACTS WON'T SET IT OFF...

BRRRAAPPP

...AND IF THEY CAN'T WALK, THEY CAN'T VERY WELL DELIVER THEIR PAYLOADS.

BRRRAAPP-KA-

BULGED-CASE JAM! CAN'T CLEAR IT WITHOUT A ROD.

AND THAT BUCKET OF BOLTS ISN'T GETTING DOWN INTO THE *PIT*...

...NOT ON *MY* WATCH!

OY! THERE'S DESTRO AND BARONESS!

I CAN DROP MY RUSE THEN.

GOOD THING. I WAS BEGINNING TO FORGET IT WAS REALLY YOU...

LET'S NOT GO THERE, BUZZER.

MOUNT UP, DREADNOKS...

...AND *RIDE!*

NICE TECHNIQUE, SNAKE EYES!

BUT THIS WHOLE ENCOUNTER WASN'T ABOUT SWORDSMANSHIP, IT WAS JUST A MEANS TO EMPLOY...

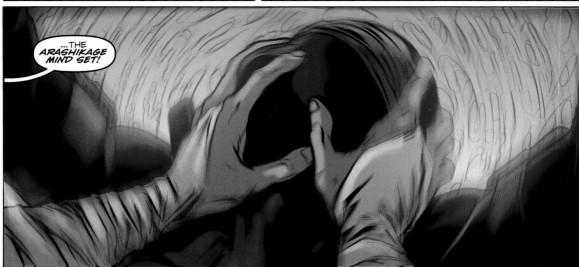

...THE ARASHIKAGE MIND SET!

HERE, IN THE CORRIDORS OF YOUR MIND, WHERE NOTHING IS HARDWIRED, AND WHERE THE ICONS CONSTRUCTED BY DR. VENOM ARE AS EPHEMERAL AS HIS MALIGN REVENANT...

...WHERE A SWITCH IS NO LONGER CONNECTED TO ITS OLD CIRCUIT, BUT IS NOW WIRED TO THE ENTIRE ALTERNATE REALITY CREATED BY THE BRAINWAVE SCANNER...

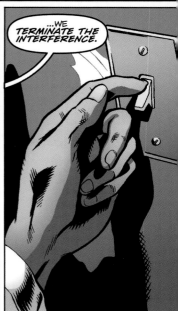

...WE TERMINATE THE INTERFERENCE.

IN UTAH, DIRECTLY ABOVE THE SECRET G.I. JOE HEADQUARTERS KNOWN AS "THE PIT".

I'M JUST RUNNING A SCAN TO MAKE SURE THERE'S NO ORDNANCE SITTING ON TOP OF THE TRAPDOOR.

THAT DOUBLE DOSE OF MK-82 PAVEWAYS THAT ACE UNLOADED ON THE COBRA B.A.T.S* PRETTY MUCH CLEARED THE DECK UP HERE, BUT IT'S PRUDENT TO MAKE EXTRA-SURE...

*BATTLE ANDROID TROOPER.

...OKAY, THIS IMMEDIATE AREA IS CLEAR. YOU AND TUNNEL RAT CAN COME UP, STALKER.

LOOK AT ALL THIS! THOSE BOMBS IMPACTED A QUARTER OF A KLICK AWAY, SO THIS IS ALL JUST DEBRIS THAT FELL OUT OF THE SKY!

WHERE'S *SPIRIT IRON KNIFE?* WE LOST TRACK OF HIM AFTER HE TACKLED THAT KAMIKAZE B.A.T.*

*LAST ISSUE.

THOSE COBRA ANDROID TROOPERS WERE PACKED FULL OF EXPLOSIVES. THEY WERE, IN EFFECT, WALKING BUNKER PENETRATORS.

TRIPWIRE, WE ARE ALL LUCKY THAT SPIRIT STOPPED ONE FROM GETTING THROUGH THE TRAPDOOR.

HIS CHANCES WEREN'T ALL THAT GOOD. THERE'S HARDLY A DEPRESSION DEEP ENOUGH TO TAKE COVER IN—

I FOUND ONE THAT WAS JUST DEEP ENOUGH.

SPIRIT!

FLATTENING OUT LOW IS THE TRICK. AND BEING LUCKY. THAT B.A.T. DETONATED LESS THAN A METER AWAY—

—BUT WE SHOULD CONTINUE THE DEBRIEF DOWN IN THE *PIT.*

DON'T YOU NEED MEDICAL TREATMENT? THE CONCUSSION MUST HAVE—

OH, I'LL BE LEACHING OUT SHRAPNEL THROUGH MY SKIN FOR A MONTH OR TWO. BUT RIGHT NOW...

...I'M MORE CONCERNED ABOUT THAT *COBRA RATTLER* COMING IN NAP-OF-THE-EARTH FROM THE FOOTHILLS.

ULP! MY SENSORS ARE ALSO PICKING UP UNEXPLODED ORDNANCE OUT HERE!

COBRA GROUND CONTROL NET—THIS IS RATTLER-SEVEN-CHARLIE. WORKING MY WAY THROUGH THE RAVINES WITH ALL SYSTEMS PASSIVE TOOK LONGER THAN EXPECTED...

...CAN YOU UPDATE ME ON THE EXACT POSITIONS OF OUR ASSETS AND B.A.T.S SO I CAN AVOID COLLATERAL DAMAGE...?

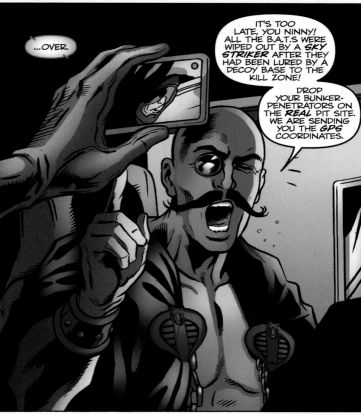

...OVER.

IT'S TOO LATE, YOU NINNY! ALL THE B.A.T.S WERE WIPED OUT BY A *SKY STRIKER* AFTER THEY HAD BEEN LURED BY A DECOY BASE TO THE KILL ZONE!

DROP YOUR BUNKER-PENETRATORS ON THE *REAL* PIT SITE. WE ARE SENDING YOU THE *GPS* COORDINATES.

A SKY STRIKER IS IN THE NABE? NOT GOOD! I CAN DELIVER MY PAYLOAD, BUT IT WILL HAVE TO BE A LOW-INGRESS, POP-UP BOMB RUN.

DUKE! THERE'S A RATTLER COMING IN LOW—

THANKS, SPIRIT—MAINFRAME ALREADY HAS A VISUAL ON IT.

IT'S PACKING *1000 LB BUNKER BUSTERS!* THAT MIGHT DO US A BIT OF DAMAGE IF THEY COME DOWN THE ELEVATOR SHAFT!

RAISE *ACE* ON THE GUARD CHANNEL. HE SHOULD STILL BE FLYING A RACETRACK *CAP** ABOVE US.

I ALREADY PATCHED HIM THROUGH.

*COMBAT AIR PATROL. A "RACETRACK" IS AN OVAL FLIGHT PATTERN.

I HEAR YOU, DUKE...

...LOOK-DOWN RADAR WILL HAVE A HARD TIME DIFFERENTIATING THE RATTLER FROM GROUND CLUTTER—

—YOU MIGHT HAVE TO ZERO ME IN ON HIM OLD-SCHOOL.

MEANWHILE IN MIDTOWN MANHATTAN.

THAT INSUFFERABLE NINJA HAS BEEN MY BANE FOR FAR TOO LONG...

...BUT SNAKE EYES AND HIS COHORT STORM SHADOW WILL NOT PREVAIL!

NOT AS LONG AS I, *DR. VENOM*, RETAIN CONTROL OF YOUNG BILLY'S BODY!

HEY! ARE YOU TWO **CRAZY?**

EVERYBODY IS BEING **EVACUATED** FROM THIS BUILDING, AND YOU'RE GOING **IN?**

WE'RE— UM—**FIRST RESPONDERS!**

OH YEAH? WHAT THE HECK KIND OF UNIFORMS ARE THOSE?

BESIDES, THERE'S NOTHING YOU CAN DO FOR THAT GUY HANGING OFF THE HELICOPTER THAT CRASHED INTO THE BUILDING...

...THAT HELICOPTER IS BALANCED PRECARIOUSLY! IF YOU TRY TO GO OUT ONTO IT TO GET HIM, IT'LL TIP RIGHT OVER! IF HE EVEN MOVES, IT'LL GO—

—WHU? WHERE'D THOSE TWO GO?

GPS COORDINATES LOADED INTO THE FLIGHT COMPUTER AND NAVIGATION HUD* IS UP. LINING UP THE TADPOLE ON THE MARKER AND WE ARE GOOD TO GO.

*HEADS-UP DISPLAY

LGBs* ARE NOW SLAVED TO THE TARGETING POD.

AND WE HAVE A LOCK.

*LASER GUIDED BOMB.

TIME TO POP UP...

...TO BOMB-RELEASE ALTITUDE.

NOWHERE TO RUN, NO PLACE TO HIDE!

CALL DUKE! WARN HIM!

WE MAY BE TOO LATE! THE CARGO POD OF THE HELICOPTER IS TEARING LOOSE!

SNAKE EYES AND STORM SHADOW!

HAVE THEY COME UP HERE TO *GLOAT?!*

I'LL GET HIM!

I WON'T GIVE THEM THE SATISFACTION!

MY ANGLE-OF-ATTACK INDICATOR SHOWS THE RATTLER IS CLIMBING STRAIGHT *UP* TOWARDS ME!

I DON'T HAVE ANY CHOICE OTHER THAN TO ENGAGE WITH AIM-7S* AND MAINTAIN RADAR LOCK!

*SPARROW RADAR GUIDED AIR-TO-AIR MISSILE.

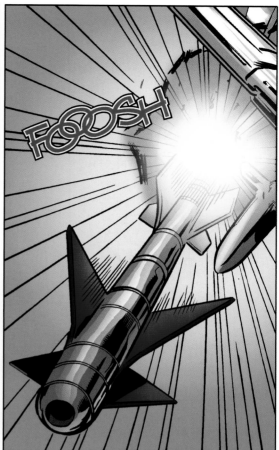

FOOOSH

MISSILE LAUNCH! THAT SKY STRIKER IS DIVING RIGHT OUT OF THE SUN!

ROLL OVER, PULL BACK ON THE STICK...

...AND POP CHAFF AND FLARES!

BLAM

UNGH!

YOU'RE NOT *BILLY!* HE WOULD KNOW TO AIM WHERE THE TARGET IS *GOING* TO BE...

...NOT WHERE IT ALREADY *IS.*

GOTTA GET YOU SORTED OUT!

BUT, *FIRST,* WE NEED TO GET CLEAR OF THIS SCRAP METAL—

WHAT ARE YOU BABBLING ABOUT?

DON'T YOU REALIZE YOU'RE *DEAD?!*

THOSE MISSILES AREN'T BEING SPOOFED BY FLARES OR CHAFF!

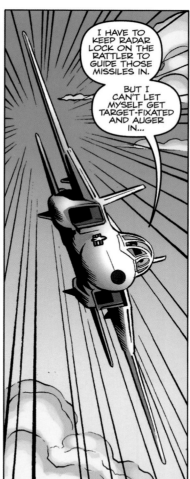

I HAVE TO KEEP RADAR LOCK ON THE RATTLER TO GUIDE THOSE MISSILES IN.

BUT I CAN'T LET MYSELF GET TARGET-FIXATED AND AUGER IN...

...PULL UP! PULL UP!

CLOSE ONE, ACE!

TOO CLOSE!

HAVE TO MAKE THOSE MISSILE SEEKER HEADS EXCEED THEIR GIMBAL LIMIT AND LOSE TRACKING!

BILLY KNOWS BETTER THAN THAT.

THE *REAL* BILLY KNOWS...

...THAT TO CONQUER FEAR IS TO CONQUER DEATH—

WHAP

UNGH!

—AND TO CONQUER DEATH, IS TO CONQUER LIFE.

SNAKE EYES! HOW—?

THE REAL BILLY WOULDN'T EXPECT AN ANSWER TO THAT.

CALLING UP THE *EEGS HUD** FOR A GUN TARGETING SOLUTION—

—GOTTA TRY FOR A SNAP-SHOT.

*ENHANCED ENVELOPE GUN SIGHT HEADS-UP DISPLAY.

UH-OH! HE'S LINING ME UP FOR A BURST OF 20 MIKE-MIKE!

BUT...

...IN ORDER TO *HIT* ME, HE HAS TO KEEP ME IN HIS SIGHTS!

AND I HAVE A MUCH TIGHTER TURNING RADIUS THAN HE HAS!

I CAN'T CUT INSIDE THAT TURN...

...BUT MY RATE OF CLIMB BEATS HIS!

HE'S PULLING *UP?*

CHUNGG

RATTLER SEVEN CHARLIE! STOP *DAWDLING!*

BLOW THE JOES TO MOLECULES WITH YOUR BUNKER-BUSTING BOMBS!

HAVE TO GAIN ALTITUDE FOR THAT...

*CONTINUOUSLY COMPUTED IMPACT POINT.

...AND SWITCH MY HUD TO CCIP* BOMBING MODE!

"POPPING UP" TO INITIATE BOMB RUN!

UH-OH! A B.A.T. EXPLOSIVE PACK HAS GONE ACTIVE AND IS COUNTING DOWN!

I'VE GOT IT.

CAREFUL! IT MIGHT HAVE A TREMBLER SWITCH!

TARGET IN LINE AND LOCKED— *UHG*—

—HERE COMES THAT SKY-STRIKER AGAIN!

HE'S *BLUFFING!* HE CAN'T SHOOT AT THIS RANGE BECAUSE HE WON'T BE ABLE TO ESCAPE THE BLAST IF HIS CANNON BURST IGNITES MY ORDNANCE!

I'M WALKING THIS PUPPY OUT OF THE AREA. WE DON'T WANT IT SETTING OFF SECONDARY EXPLOSIONS NEAR THE *PIT* IF IT GOES OFF.

UM... DON'T BREATHE TOO HARD ON IT—

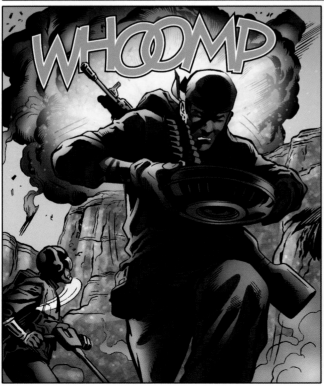

WHOOMP

—HOLY SMOKE! THAT WAS THE *RATTLER* BLOWING UP! BUT WHERE'S THE *SKY STRIKER?*

ARRRRGH!

THUMP

UNF!

THWACK

AK!

NICE MOVE. NEVER SEEN THE *ARASHIKAGE DEATH TOUCH* EXECUTED IN NON-LETHAL MODE BEFORE...

...AFTER ALL IS SAID AND DONE, THAT WAS THE EASY PART.

NOW, COMES THE HARD PART.

WAIT! ONE PLANE SURVIVED THAT BLAST...

...THE SKY STRIKER!

WAY TO GO, ACE!

YOWCH!

KINDA JUMPY, HUH?

I LAID THE PACKAGE DOWN WHERE IT'S SAFE. BUT WE STILL NEED TO SEND THE EOD* ROBOT UP HERE TO DO A SWEEP.

*EXPLOSIVE ORDINANCE DISPOSAL.

WHAT TOOK YOU GUYS SO LONG?

108

DID YOU HEAR THAT?

I THOUGHT I SAW SOMETHING ZIP ACROSS THE CEILING LIKE *DRACULA!* AND THEN, I WAS SURE I HEARD THE BASEMENT DOOR OPENING!

WHY WOULD ANYBODY WANT TO GO TO THE BASEMENT? NOTHING THERE...

"...OTHER THAN THE *BRAINWAVE SCANNER.*"

THERE'S NO WAY YOU CAN EXPUNGE ME FROM BILLY! YOU WOULD HAVE TO USE MY OWN MEMORIES AGAINST ME, AND YOU DON'T KNOW ENOUGH ABOUT ME!

WE'LL SEE ABOUT THAT.

ZZZZAPP

UNHHH...

SCARED, HUH? YOU SHOULD BE, DR. VENOM...

...DO YOU KNOW WHO THAT DEAD MAN IN THE KAYAK IS? DO YOU RECOGNIZE HIS WEASEL SKULL NECKLACE?

K-KWINN!

HE NO LONGER HAS A VOICE, BUT HE'S CALLING FOR YOU.

HE WANTS YOU TO DRIFT THROUGH THE ICY WATERS OF ETERNITY WITH HIM.

NOOOO!

YOU CAN'T LET THIS—THIS—THING CARRY ME OFF!

MERCY! HAVE MERCY— PLEASE...

AIIIIIIIII!

YOU'LL HAVE TO WORK THAT OUT WITH KWINN. THAT'S NOT UP TO US TO DISPENSE.

I FEEL LIKE I JUST WOKE UP FROM A HORRIBLE DREAM...

YOU DID.

BUT FOR SOMEBODY ELSE, THE NIGHTMARE IS JUST BEGINNING.

THE STORY CONTINUES IN OUR NEXT VOLUME!

ART GALLERY

CAPT. ARMBRUSTER

MSGT. TRIMPE - CREW CHIEF

G.I.JOE

A REAL AMERICAN HERO

VOLUME 2